The Petulant Owl a̶ ̶ ̶ ̶ ̶ ̶ ̶ ̶ ̶ re NonSuch Poems

Florence Remmer

Published by PublishingPush.com

ACKNOWLEDGEMENTS

To my great great Nephew and Nieces
Tyler Maisie Ruby and Emma

From Florence

CONTENTS

A TALE FROM THE LAUNDRY MICE

I had a call from the Belfry Bats,
Long standing friends of mine,
Asking could they sleep the night
On my washing line?

Apparently the Belfry Mice
Were putting on a show
And, needing all the belfry space,
They'd asked the Bats to go

T'was a one night only fashion show..
..Oh, would I be so good
To house them for that single night?
Well of course I would!

I pegged them gently on the line,
A' snoozing side by side,
The fashion show went with a swing
And all were satisfied.

A MOST GRATEFUL SCARECROW

That very kind Mouse with a penny to spare
Decided to spend it on ME!!!!!!!

She bought a long bun in a crinkly bag
And sent it, with love, for my tea!

Such kindness deserves
a gift in return
Of that there is nary a doubt!

So I'll dig up a turnip for kindly Miss Mouse
(I don't care if the farmer finds out)

JENNY WREN, WILY BIRD...

…reads the tea leaves
So I've heard.
Tells you what you want to know
For £1 or 2 or so

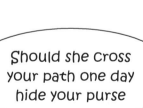

If you are poor then Wily Jenny
Will read one tea leaf
For one penny

Should she cross
your path one day
hide your purse

Solo tea leaf, solo penny
All is grist
To wily Jenny

A BLUSH OF SHAME

A poor but honest
Country Mouse
Found full twenty pence!

She put it in
Her handbag
(She couldn't help herself)

She felt her cheeks
Blush red with shame,
Her heart began to pound

So she wrote a little
'Thank you' note
And pinned it to the ground.

DEAR EXHAUSTED SALMON...

…all that frantic
Upstream leaping!
All that toil
To be
Ahead!

Why don't you start
From up the top
And wisely
Swim downstream
Instead?

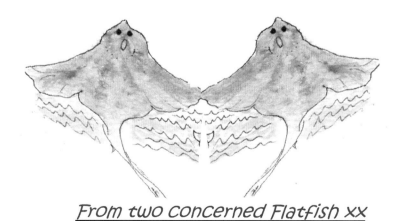

From two concerned Flatfish xx

CAR BOOT SALE

Three little mice with carrier bags
A' standing in the rain
Asked me if I'd ANYTHING
For their car boot sale

I gave them fourteen whistles,
Two drums and an old brass gong
They put them in their carrier bags,
Thanked me, and moved on

Now, a blackbird bought the whistles,

A rooster, the old brass gong

And I'm told a March hare bought the drums
To practice **thumping on**

Thump!!

8

THE CARPENTER CAT

A carpenter cat
Decided one day
To fit wooden doors on the mouse holes

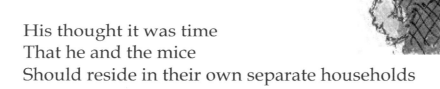

His thought it was time
That he and the mice
Should reside in their own separate households

He fit solid doors
(And sealed them no less),
The mice felt left out….they felt slighted

So…they packed up their bags
And went off in their droves

And the carpenter cat was delighted

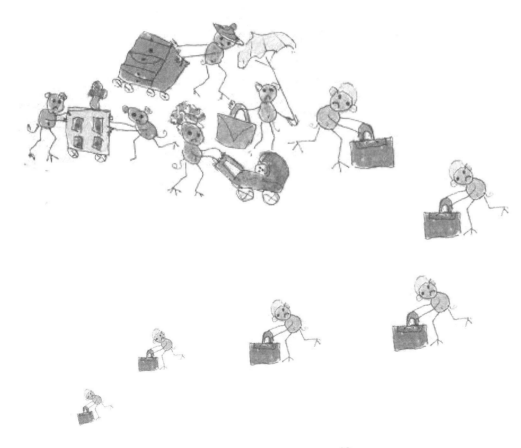

CHEESE FOR DINNER

Sometimes the moon
Is big and round
Sometimes he looks much thinner

And that's the time
Our friends all know
We're having cheese for dinner

O Mr. Moon
Is very kind
He says he really doesn't mind
Providing cheese for dinner

He slips away when the sun comes out
He goes through a starry door
And he eats all day in the Milky Way
That's how he gets round once more

Full of yummy cheese please

CHESHIRE CAT

Oh, Cheshire cat, dear Cheshire cat
Will you accompany me?
For I'm going
To the market
To see what I can see.

I can't accompany you, Miss Mouse
Though it's kind of you to ask me
I have to stay
Indoors today
Because I've lost my false teeth

Oh, Cheshire cat, dear Cheshire cat
I have a good idea
I've an old piano
In my house
Let's go and take the ivories out..
  ...and make you a new set, dear!!!!!

We'll file them down
A little bit
I'm sure they'll be
A perfect fit
Then you can go to market

(the false teeth looked so very nice,
but frightened all the scary mice)
Te hee

Aghh!

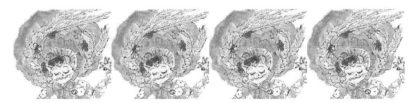

THE CHESHIRE CAT'S TALE

I run a small Tea Shop in Cheshire
My clients are chic and refined
They say "thank you" and "please"
When they sample my cheese
And leave tips of a generous kind

FRIENDS

A lettuce filled Rabbit
With nothing to do
Decided to hop for an hour or two
A friendly young Frog
Then decided that he
Would hop with the Rabbit to keep company
Oh they hopped and they laughed
In the friendliest way,
And made plans
to meet for a hop every day
And soon… hopping became
A regular habit
Twixt the friendly young Frog
 and the lettuce filled Rabbit

THE CYCLIST'S TALE

…I found an empty Tortoise shell
One morning, whilst out riding
I wondered where the owner was
And where he may be hiding

A passing Spider and his wife
Smiled at my concern
"Why he's stepped out for a breather, sir,
Pray wait for his return"

IMPORTANT ADVICE

When your Grandma
Comes to tea
Be as truthful as can be

'Cos Grandmamas
Are very wise
They look at you with knowing eyes

Now Grandmas can
Be lots of fun
They never tell on anyone

They give you hugs
And dry your tears
And understand your little fears

But never tell your
Grandma lies!!!!!
Remember…she has knowing eyes
(you will have them too, one day)

HAPPY BIRTHDAY, TORTOISE

The Birthday Fairy came along
And whispered in my ear
"What wish may I be granting you
Now your birthdays near"

"Thank you" I shyly answered,
"And the thing I'd like the most
Is a brand new shiny letter box
So I can have some post

Happy
birthday, Mr T

This house of mine is warm as socks
But doesn't have a letter box.!

"Ah yes", replied the fairy
"This I will gladly do
Then folks can bring you presents
And post their cards to you".

THE INDEPENDENT SHEEP

Two very independent Sheep
(Far between and few)
Removed their woolly coats themselves
The day the shearing man was due

The very grateful shearing man
With two less fleece to reap
Gave a warm red jackets each ….
…to those thoughtful Sheep

SHORT CHANGED BY A PEA

Four sibling Mice
Sat down for tea
As greedy as four Mice can be
One Mouse counted
On his plate
Nine peas; the others each had eight

One Mouse, smirking,
Ate his tea
The others sulked throughout the meal
The others sulked
In misery
To be Oh! short changed by one pea

(A note to mothers everywhere
Make sure your babies have fair share)

WISE OWLS

A Phoenix bird set off one day
To probe the ozone layer

Folks warned him of the danger
He didn't seem to care
Folks saw him rise and fly away
Folks waved a last fare well
But we say he'll return one day
With quite a tale to tell

signed by the owls

NIHIL CONOR NIHIL ACQUIRO

LEMUR LOOK

A business-like Lemur with hypnotic eyes
Placed an ad. in a magazine page
He wagered £1 to anyone who
Could out stare his spell binding gaze

He had lots of replies from various folk,
Moles, rabbits etc. and mice
They all lost the wager, 'cos no one dare look
For long, at those trancy filled eyes

'Til one day a Peacock a' challenged the bet
(Crowds gathered to watch,
so they say)
..he smiled as he spread out his feathery tail
An eye catching, eyeful display…..

…They tell me the Lemur, when faced with the sight,
(Not knowing on which eye to gaze),
Lowered his lids!!!
Oh his wager was lost!
He paid up and went home in a daze

THE PETULANT OWL

A petulant Owl
Once took a chance
And decided to ask
Miss Mouse For a Dance

When she declined
(with tact and great charm)
He sulked for three months
And one week In his barn

Yes he sulked in his barn
For three month and one week
That foot tapping Owl
With the Petulant Streak.

Sulky
owl

A SAD FISHY TALE

An eccentric
Young Gold Fish
Full of false pride

Decided to
Show off
And swim on his side!

But I'm sorry
To add…
At the end of the day

Someone thought
He had died
And threw him away.

LACKADAY

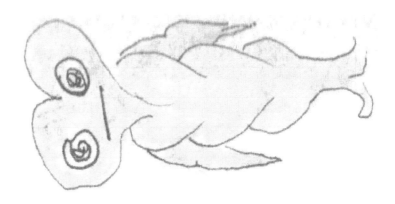

MANNY.CURIST

W.W.W.
Answer this e-mail if anyone knows
The best way to varnish
Miss cats hidden claws?
Manny.Curist@ditdotcom

Dear Manny,
Well, you must be very crafty
Of that there is no doubt
And bribe a mouse to taunt Miss Cat
Until her claws fly out

Then, moving very fast dear,
Give the claws a shine
Miss Cat will thank you kindly
And pay you for your time

The mouse will kindly thank you
For his little bit of fun
And that dear, in a nutshell,
Is how the deed is done.
Cheers, V.crafty@mouseville.com

SCHOOL OF BALLET...FREE LESSONS

Look at the Ballet dancer
Dancing on one toe
How does she keep her balance?
That's what we'd like to know!

Please teach us how to dance upon one toe …

…we want to know!

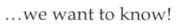

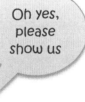

THE SNAIL AND THE CENTIPEDE

The Snail is such a lucky bod
He only has one foot to shod

One foot to shod…unlike the poor
Centipede with nigh five score

POPPY THE CAT

What would you do
If you had a cat
And you said to that cat "I love you'…

And the cat replied,
with knowing eyes,
" I know…and I love you too"
Oh my, what would you do?

Would you stroke him with a smile
Or would you scream and run a mile?

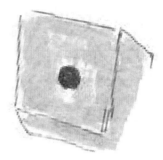

SNAKE EYES

Will snakes become offended
When they finally realize
White dice, with a dot on,
Are likened to their eyes?

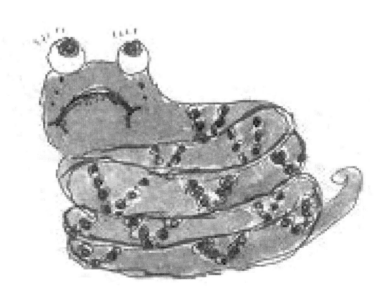

TWO PONDEROUS DILEMMAS FOR A VET

An itching scratching Sheep
A spotty itching Gull

One allergic to fish from the sea!!!

t'other allergic to wool!!!

TALKING IN HIS SLEEP?

A mouse was talking in his sleep
You know,…re. this and that,
And listening at the keyhole
Was a nosey grinning cat.

Aye, listening in the darkness
Creased up in silent glee…
…when through the keyhole filtered
"Cash" "hidden" "old oak tree"

The cat's sly eyes flew open
Oh! his heart began to thud
  As he set off running (spade in hand)
To the local oak tree wood.

I think I heard the sleeping mouse
Ramble on some more…
…"cat" "been" "had" "again"…but O,
I really can't be sure…..

THE FAIRY SALE

Suppose you were invited
To a sale of MAGIC THINGS,
Of hats of invisibility
Of cars and boots with wings

Of books with talking pictures…
..which you could step inside!
Of never ending bowls of sweets
Tell me, what would YOU buy?

Or, maybe, for a few pence more
A trip behind a MAGIC DOOR…
..to buy a magic dream, oh my
Tell me…what WOULD you buy?
Really? And so would I

THE KNITTER

Poor little Spider
Don't know how to spin
Her mother never taught her
And that's an awful sin
Has to earn her living
Knitting for a Cat

Knit one, pearl one
Just fancy that!

Hats and gloves and mittens
For a Dandy cat

THE THREE GENTEEL PIGS

Three Genteel Pigs, oh genteel indeed,
Appalled at the way they were given their feed
Appalled at the food and the lack of finesse
Decided to hire an outside cateress

So they hired one Miss Mouse, a baker by trade,
(who put currants galore in the pasties she made)
Yes they hired Bakeress Mouse for 3 pennies a day
To serve them their meals on a silvery tray

With china and napkins, you know, things like that
All served by Miss Mouse in a waitressy hat
And the three Genteel Pigs were delighted to pay..
….for finesse and refinement, three pennies a day

WEEPING WILLOW?

O, Weeping Willow, why do you weep so?
Why all the sighing
when the wind blows through your hair?

"Oh thank you for asking…
let me tell you why I weep so
And why I start a 'sighing
when the breeze blows here and there

Soft breezes sing their songs
And blow secrets in my ear
And the sun shines through my waving leaves
And I Sigh and Weep with Joy …my dears.

So lovely

A WELL EARNED SIXPENCE

When you have a loose tooth
And it finally drops out,
Have you ever wondered
What the fuss is all about?

Why put it 'neath the pillow?
Why not just throw it away?
Why do the Fairies want it?
Well….I'll tell you if I may…

…A little Baby sometimes cries
Because he wants a tooth

(When they're born they have none
That's the honest truth)

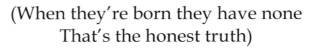

So the Fairies come
And take your tooth
(Leave sixpence for your pain)

They put it in the
Babies mouth
To make him smile again.

A WIDE AWAKE CRAFTY CAT

Six Mice were sat on a doorstep,
Squabbling (as they do),
When the cat flap opened with a bang
And a sleeping Cat marched through…

…he sleep marched past the startled Mice
Then turning, sleep marched back,
And the cat flap closed behind him
With a great resounding smack

The spooked out Mice fast scarpered!
Silence reigned once more
And the crafty Cat laughed loudly
Behind the cat flap door

THE ASTONISHING TALE OF A PEREGRINE FALCON

A Peregrine
Was flying home
Beneath a stormy sky
When, to his
Great astonishment,
Two cats went whizzing by…

Now, the cats had been
A' roofing
When suddenly their tails…
…Were caught up in
The weathervane
(The wind was blowing gales!)

Spinning out
The cats were flung
Into the hurricane
And apart from one
Astonished bird
Were never seen again.

THE WISE AND CAUTIOUS RABBIT

I met a twisting Tumbling Flea
'I've quit my job
At the circus', says he

'And what will you do for your wages', says I
'None of your business',
Says he, looking sly.

'No,! none of your business',
says he with a leap
'But I'm looking for lodgings
Somewhere to sleep'.

'Oh you're so right
'tis none of my business', says I
And scurried away
Without saying goodbye

Oh what a performance!
Oh what an itchycoo day
Lock up your dog and your moggies
He's looking for somewhere to stay

THE TADPOLE

One little Tadpole
Washed and dressed
All done up in his Sunday best
Hair brushed back
Eyes agog
His time has come to be a Frog

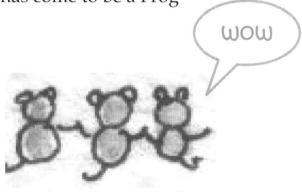

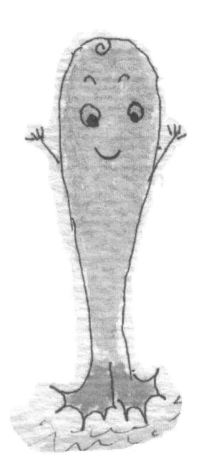

Two new legs
Soon filled the void
One little Tadpole overjoyed

WISHFUL THINKING

(of a very very old Cat)

An old Tom cat
Sat by a stream
A' fishing for his supper

He caught two kippers
On his line
And then he caught another

"Tasty kippers!
Yum Yum Yum
It's what I've been a' wishing!"

He licked his lips
Two hundred times
Then carried on a' fishing.

THE WEAVER OF DREAMS

A cat once dreamed the same dull dream
Five nights in a row…
And he sent a letter of complaint
To let the Weaver know

The Weaver, by return of post
 (With much apology),
Sent a parcel firm filled with
The most fantastic dreams…

…of chasing mice, scraps, brawls et al
What cat could ask for more?
And he penned a letter of content
To let the Weaver know.

A THOUGHTFUL FRIEND

O Mistress Hooting Tooting Owl
Will you tell me truly
Why you hoot
The whole night long
Why don't you go to bed dear?

Dear Mistress Mouse I must confess
The reason I hoot nightly
And why I cannot
Go to bed
Well….I do not have a nightie

O Mistress Hooting Tooting owl
That's very sad to hear
Look… if it helps you
Sleep tonight
Pray borrow one of mine dear!

Printed in Poland
by Amazon Fulfillment
Poland Sp. z o.o., Wrocław

24960551R00038